The Genie

by Mary Hooper

Illustrated by Kirstin Holbrow

You do not need to read this page – just get on with the book!

Published in 2003 in Great Britain by
Barrington Stoke Ltd
10 Belford Terrace, Edinburgh EH4 3DQ

This edition based on *The Genie*, published by Barrington Stoke in 1999

ISBN 1-84299-120-5

Printed by Polestar AUP Aberdeen Ltd

Meet The Author - Mary Hooper

What is your favourite animal?

A cat

What is your favourite boy's name?

Rowan

What is your favourite girl's name?

Bethany (this week!)

What is your favourite food?

Seafood

What is your favourite music?

Rolling Stones

What is your favourite hobby?

Pottering about

Meet The Illustrator - Kirstin Holbrow

What is your favourite animal?

My dog, Pewter Plum

What is your favourite boy's name?

George

What is your favourite girl's name?

Beryl

What is your favourite food?

Shellfish

What is your favourite music?

Ambient Techno

What is your favourite hobby?

Rowing on the River Wye

Contents

This is me, Fudge
This is my sister, Sarah
F

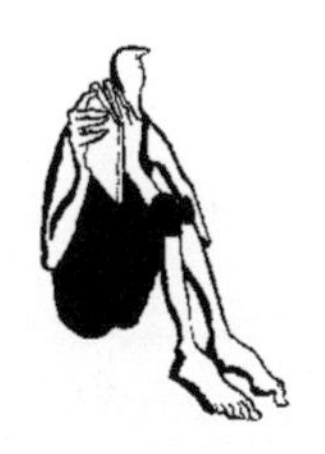

Chapter 1
Dad's Birthday Present

My sister Sarah and I were at a jumble sale. It was our dad's birthday soon. We were both broke, so we'd gone there to find a present for him.

"Hey, Fudge, have you found anything yet?" Sarah asked me, looking at a table full of junk.

There were chipped mugs, old plastic plates and rusty tin trays.

"Nothing," I said. "Not a thing."

"Ha!" Sarah said. "I've just seen something ..."

She started to explore the next stall along.

I stared at all that junk. Then I saw a small box. It was dark blue, with a silver moon on the top and stars all over. Would Dad like it? I picked it up.

Maybe ...

"Do you want that, dear?" said the woman behind the stall. "You can have it for 20p."

"I'll take it!" I said.

I paid and moved away to look at the box more closely. I lifted the lid. Inside was a scrap of paper with this message:

To call out the spirit of the box – tap G-E-N-I-E in Morse code.

To send him back, tap GENIE backwards – E-I-N-E-G ...

What did *that* mean? It must be some sort of joke.

BRIC A BRAC

"What's that tatty old thing?" Sarah asked me.

"What do you think it is?" I snapped.

Sarah and I don't get on. She's a year older than me, and she tries to push me around.

"It looks like a dirty old box," Sarah said. "Have you got *that* for Dad?"

"Perhaps," I replied.

"Well, how mean can you get?" Sarah smiled. "What do you think I've got him? The *best* present! Something fantastic!"

She held up a big clumsy thing. "A trouser press! He's always wanted one."

"Big deal," I said.

"And you've got him that *old box thing*?" she said. "Well, he won't like that but he's going to *love* what I've got."

"Well, hooray for you," I said.

Chapter 2
A Sight for Sore Eyes?

Two days later I was sitting at my desk in my bedroom. It was homework time but I had *The Wonderful World of Knowledge* out on my bed. And it was open at the page with the Morse code.

I wasn't planning to do anything about the message on that scrap of paper in the box.

I was doing my homework. Sarah and I were in the same history group in our school and had the same homework to do – we had to write three pages on 'Schools in Victorian England'. Of course she'd done hers.

I looked at the blue box on my desk and thought *what if ...*

I told myself not to be silly.

Yes, but what if ...

There was no harm in having a go ...

Before I could stop myself, I picked up the box. I looked in *The Wonderful World of Knowledge* to find the letters G-E-N-I and E

in Morse code. Then I tapped them on the lid of the box.

I felt a bit silly. I was just about to go back to my homework, when there was a sparky noise and a puff of smoke. There was an odd smell like cheap perfume too.

mini Garden
FUDGE'S FOLDER
KEEP OUT
GENIE
How did that happen?

And then a voice said, “Oh, dearie me. Some mistake. This isn’t a palace in Arabia.”

I jumped. There he was, a fat little man with a bright blue cloak and puffy trousers. He had long pointed shoes with bells on them and lots of gold chains and rings. He looked like a cross between a wizard and a circus clown.

“Who are you?” we both said at once.

He bowed low. “I am the Genie of the Box.”

“D-don’t be silly,” I said. “You can’t be!”

“I am,” he said. “And who are you ...?”

“Fiona,” I told him. “They call me Fudge.”

“Princess Fiona?” he asked.

“No. Just Miss.”

He looked puzzled. “I work for Princes and Princesses, most of the time,” he said.

He looked round at the mess in my bedroom – at the torn wallpaper, the apple cores on the floor and the dirty mugs on my desk. He looked even more puzzled.

“I work in grand palaces and lofty castles,” he said.

“S-sorry,” I said. “This time you’ve got me and 12 Arnott Avenue. I live here with my sister Sarah and my dad.”

“And have you got 200 servants?” he asked.

I shook my head.

“No room,” I said.

This was crazy. It must be some mad dream.

But at the same time, a bit of me was thinking that if he was a genie, wow, how fantastic! A genie could get me things, jewels and gold and a red sports car and *anything*. He could take me for a ride on a magic carpet, grant me three wishes …

“Are you a real genie?” I asked.

He bowed deeply. “I am, oh Princess. May your camels never go lame …” He stopped and looked around. “That’s a bit over the top for you, isn’t it? I mean, have you ever seen a real live camel?”

“I saw one at London Zoo, two years ago,” I told him.

Three wishes, I was thinking. *A nice present for Dad, some fantastic outfits for me, and a mountain bike. That was it!*

"Is it true that genies can grant people three wishes?" I asked.

"Of course, oh Princess," said Genie, with another bow.

"Great!" I said. "Three wishes! Can I have them now, please?"

"Just as you wish, oh Princess."

"Thanks a lot," I said. Having a genie around was going to be OK ...

Chapter 3
Wish Upon a Star ...

I was just about to tell him my three wishes when Genie clapped his hands. There was a big puff of smoke and oops – there were three ugly old women in tall black hats in my room. They had dark cloaks and broomsticks. I gave a yell.

"Here are your three witches, oh Princess!" said the Genie.

The three witches gave a horrid laugh.

“By eye of toad and cat’s botty …” one began.

“Not *witches*,” I cried. “Wishes. I said three *wishes*!”

“Oh, dearie me,” said the Genie. “Do you wish to get rid of them?”

“Yes, please!”

“All three of them? You don’t want to keep one for spells and magic?”

“No, thank you.”

“You’ll have used up two of your three wishes, you know.”

“That doesn’t matter,” I said. “But please be quick.” One witch was rubbing her hands together and looking as if she'd like to put me into her pot.

Genie looked a bit put out, but he clapped his hands. All three of them vanished. There was nothing left but the smell of wood smoke.

I sat down on my bed, feeling faint.

"Do you want your last wish now, oh Princess?" Genie asked.

"Just give me a second ..."

Just as I was thinking about whether to have a mountain bike or a present for Dad, my door was flung open.

There stood Sarah.

She looked at me, looked at him, and yelled. “What’s that awful little fat man doing here?”

“He’s er ... just a friend!” I told her.

"That's not a friend! That's a ... a genie!" And she yelled again.

"Can't you do something?!" I said to Genie. "This is my sister and she's going to make an awful fuss. My dad will find you and you'll never get back in that box again."

Genie pointed his little finger at Sarah. There was a flash and some sparks and Sarah went silent. She was still there in the doorway and her mouth was open, but not a sound came out.

"Wh ... what's up?" I asked. "She looks as if she's been frozen."

"Almost, oh Princess," said Genie. "I've freeze-framed her."

He gave a little bow. "It's the latest thing. All the rage with genies just now."

"You don't say ..." I said. I felt quite faint.

Chapter 4
A Close Shave

I waved my hand in front of Sarah's face. She didn't even blink.

"Do you want her to stay like this?" Genie asked. "It would serve her right for calling me an awful little fat man."

That would be nice, I thought. *I wouldn't have her on my back all the time. The teachers at school couldn't say, 'it's such a pity you're not more like your sister' and stuff like that.*

But then it would be hard to explain why I had a sister freeze-framed in the doorway of my bedroom.

"No," I said with a sigh. "You'd better unfreeze her."

"Do you want to go back in time to the moment she opened the door?"

I nodded. "That would be good."

"We have all the up-to-date tricks," said Genie. "We are most hip."

"But you'll have to go back in the box first, or she'll see you again."

He nodded and gave a bow. “Before I do so,” he said, “is there any other job you wish me to do for you?”

“I’m not sure,” I said. I didn’t want to use up my last wish too fast. “Are jobs the same as wishes?” I asked.

Genie shook his head. “Jobs are just dull jobs,” he said. “Like moving palaces over mountains or turning seas into gold – that’s what a job is.”

“Oh, I see,” I said. But in fact I didn’t see.

Fantastic goings-on might be OK in fairy stories but they would be hard to hide in 12 Arnott Avenue. It was going to be hard to explain where a new mountain bike had come from. And how could I tell Dad that we were going to live in a 300-room castle?

"Perhaps just a *small* job to start with," I said. "Could you write me three pages on 'Schools in Victorian England'?"

Genie pointed his little finger. There was a tiny flash and a puff of smoke. "Done!"

"Brilliant." I looked over at Sarah, frozen in the doorway. "And now her ..."

Genie pointed. "I'll make that happen a bit later, oh Princess," he said. "Now get me back in the box."

I picked up *The Wonderful World of Knowledge*. "Thank you very much. I'll call you up again soon," I said. *Just as soon as I've worked out what I want for my last wish,* I thought.

I tapped out GENIE backwards on the lid, E-I-N-E-G, in Morse code. There was a puff of smoke and Genie got smaller and smaller until he vanished into the box. He left behind him just a wisp of smoke and a spark.

A few seconds later, Sarah began to move.

"What's that?!" she said.

"What's what?"

She looked around, puzzled.

"Er ... just what's ... er ... *something* ..." She wasn't making sense. "I can't think what I was going to say."

"It's all that homework you do," I said. "It's bad for your brain."

"And why are you reading *The Wonderful World of Knowledge*? I've never seen you even look at it before."

"There's a lot you don't know about me," I said. "I'm a very private person."

She looked around the room again. "There's something funny going on ..."

"I should go and have a nice lie down," I told her.

"I was going to ask you about Dad's birthday. You're not giving him that old box, are you?"

I looked at the blue box. "No," I said. "I thought I'd get him a tape for the car."

"Well, as an extra present, I thought we could both do some jobs round the house for a week."

"OK, OK," I said. I just wanted her to go. "You sort it out and make a list."

With Genie around, the jobs would be no problem.

Sarah is always
Miss Perfect

Chapter 5
A Little Language Trouble

Sarah looked fresh, neat and tidy as we walked to school. I tugged at my jumper so that it went baggy. Sarah makes me *want* to look a mess.

"Now, here's the list of jobs," she said. "I've ticked all the ones I'm going to do."

I looked at her list. She'd chosen all the best ones, of course, like the shopping.

I'd got the awful ones like changing the sheets on the beds and doing the washing.

I stuffed the list into my school bag.

"Have you done your homework?" Sarah asked.

"Course I have!"

"Mine's really good," she said. "I'll get an A+ for it."

"Big deal," I said.

I gave in my homework that morning and forgot all about it till later.

In the afternoon, our teacher, Hoppy, was marking our homework, when she yelled out my name.

"Fiona!" she shouted. Just like that.

I stood up.

"What's this?" she asked, waving my homework at me.

"Er … three pages on 'Schools in Victorian England'?" I said.

"It could be," Hoppy said. "But why is it written in another language?"

"Is it?"

"Don't get clever with me, young lady. You've handed in three pages written in Arabic."

"Ah," I said. I was in a panic now. Genie had done my homework, but he'd done it in his own language!

I had a quick think. "Er … I hurt my hand at the weekend and my cousin wrote this for me," I told Hoppy.

"And he's an Arab, is he?"

I nodded. I didn't look at Sarah. But not even she would rat on me to a teacher.

"And is your cousin 200 years old?"

"What?"

"This is written in a very *old* form of Arabic."

"He ... er ... my cousin thought you'd like it."

"I like homework I can read," she said. "Stay in after school every night until you've done it."

****

Sarah was on at me for the rest of the day. She wanted to see my homework. In the end I had to flush it down the loo.

When at last I got home, I ran upstairs, got Genie out of the box and told him about the Arabic.

“I am so very sorry, Princess,” he said, with a bow. “May all my camels die!”

“Well, never mind all that,” I said. “But can you just do some jobs around the house for me when I’m at school tomorrow?”

“Of course, Princess!”

“I’ve got to rush now,” I said, “but I want you to dust the rooms and change the beds. Is that OK?”

“No problem, Princess!”

"Oh, and make Dad a nice birthday cake too, please."

I tapped him back into the box just in time, because Sarah looked in at my door.

"Were you talking to someone?"

"No," I said, "I was just saying a poem to myself."

"I thought I heard *two* voices!" Sarah sniffed. "And there's a funny smell of smoke."

"I just lit a match or two," I said.

"Hmm," she said and sniffed again. "Something very funny is going on around here ..."

Chapter 6
All Change

I was late home again the next day because I had to do my homework. Sarah wasn't there, she'd gone home with a friend. And that was just as well.

I went into the sitting room, looked round and gave a yelp. The room had been dusted all right, *dusted with gold dust!* It lay thick over everything. The sofa and chairs and even the goldfish bowl glowed with gold!

I shut the sitting room door behind me and ran into my bedroom.

Or tried to. I couldn't get in, because there was a bed in the way. Not my bed, but a huge new bed with thick wooden posts at each corner and a frilly roof. It had a sickly green and gold cover with jewels on.

I rushed to Sarah's room. *Her* bed was now a great hammock, with thick fur rugs and four stuffed bears at the corners.

Dad's bright blue bed was lifted high in the air, on top of four tall marble pillars.

Change the beds, I'd told the Genie. *Dust the rooms*.

And that's just what he'd done.

I ran back to my room and tapped the box.

At once, Genie was there, on my new bed. “Yes, oh Princess!” he said.

“Those jobs around the house!” I panted.

“My work is fantastic, is it not, Princess?” he said.

“Oh, it’s fantastic all right,” I said, “but you’ve got it all wrong.”

And I told him how you dust a room and change a bed.

“I must have our old beds back,” I said.

Genie looked cross. “As you wish, oh Princess,” he sniffed, and in a moment, I was lying on my old bed.

“Are *all* the beds back?” I asked. “And has the gold dust gone?”

He nodded. He was still cross.

I tapped him back into his box. Just then, there was a yell.

"Fiona!" Sarah shouted. "This cake! Where ever did you get it?"

The cake? I hadn't even looked at it.

"I made it!" I said, rushing down.

I went into the kitchen. Shock! Horror!

What's this then?
Birthday Grithing
to Father of
Fudge ~ Keeper
of the Genie

The cake was as big as a double bed. It was the sort of cake you'd make if you had asked 3,000 people to tea. It was iced in blue and green with silver balls and sweets on it. On the top, it said, BIRTHDAY GRITTINGS TO FATHER OF FUDGE, KEEPER OF THE GENIE.

"I don't understand! What's this all about ..." said Sarah.

"Ah," I said, "just wait a moment."

And then I had to dash up, get Genie out of the box and get him to freeze-frame Sarah. Then he had to change the cake into a small jam one, and so on.

I tell you, I was worn out.

Chapter 7
A Gigantic Problem

"We don't wear belly dancing outfits to parties here," I told Genie a few days later.

I'd asked Genie to find me an outfit to wear for a meal out on Dad's birthday. The one he chose was made of beads and tassels and not much else.

"But it was a most hip outfit!" Genie told me. "My other Princesses have ..."

"Well, it isn't right for round here," I said. "And now, I have to go and change the goldfish."

Genie's eyes gleamed. "Change it for a shark?"

"Change its water!" I said, with a sigh. "Goldfish are so boring. I'd like a more interesting pet."

Sarah yelled up from the kitchen that I had to go and help with the washing-up *now*. So I tapped Genie back into the box and went down.

I had to dry, of course. Then Sarah said I had to peel the potatoes. I was just going to make a fuss when I heard a funny noise from up in my room. An odd noise. Like the trumpeting of an elephant.

"What was *that*?" Sarah asked, shocked.

"Er ... was it thunder?"

"No, it wasn't thunder. It sounded like an animal. It sounded like ..."

The trumpeting came again.

"I'll go up!" I said. *What had Genie done now?* "Perhaps ... er ... one of my books has fallen off the shelf."

I rushed up to my bedroom. I couldn't get in – an elephant's bottom was in the way!

"What *is* it?" Sarah called up to me.

"Oh ... er ... next door's cat's in here," I said. "He's been jumping about and er ... making a noise. I'll catch him. Here, pussy, pussy!"

I crept between the elephant's legs and tapped the Genie out of the box.

"What's all this?" I yelled as soon as I saw him. "What's this elephant doing in my room?"

"Not a lot at the moment," Genie said. "It can't move."

"But why is it here?" I yelled. "I never asked for an elephant."

"You wished for a new pet, oh Princess," said Genie. "It was such a large wish that it took a long time to come."

"But I didn't know I had made another wish! And what sort of person has an elephant for a pet?"

"A *Princess* kind of person," Genie said.

"Oh," I said.

The elephant moved its bottom and pushed me across the room.

"Look," I said, "I'm sorry about this, but I'm not a Princess kind of person at all. This is not the pet for me."

"Do you wish me to send it back?" Genie asked in a cross voice.

"Yes, please," I said. I patted a bit of elephant. "It's very nice, of course, but no good in a small bedroom."

"I see," said Genie.

"Fiona!" Sarah's voice came from outside my door. "Why can't I get in? What's up?"

"Nothing! It's all OK. I'm just putting the cat out of the window – *here, puss*," and added so softly that only Genie could hear, "get rid of that elephant *now*, please."

Still looking very cross, Genie held up both hands to the elephant. There was a fizzing sound and a puff of smoke and it vanished.

I began to tap Genie back into his box. "Sorry," I said to him. "It was a nice thought. But I just haven't got the room."

Genie gave a bow. "Such a large wish," he said. "Anything left of the elephant will go over the next few days."

"What d'you mean?" I asked.

But he'd gone.

"It can't just be the cat!" Sarah said crossly from outside.

And then she fell through the door. She picked herself up, looked about her and gave a yell.

It was only then that I understood what Genie had said about taking a few days to go. You see, the elephant's head and trunk hadn't gone. They were floating over my desk.

The rest of the elephant was nowhere to be seen.

Chapter 8
Dream Time?

"It was just a dream," I said to Sarah the next morning. I laughed. "How *could* there have been an elephant in my bedroom? Or even a bit of an elephant?"

"It was awful!" Sarah said. "I can't go into your room now."

How can I explain this?

"That's good ... er ... that's all right," I said. "I should keep out of there for a few days."

I'd had an awful time with her the night before. I'd had to get Genie to freeze-frame her, then put her into her room. I told her it was all just a bad dream.

She mustn't tell Dad. I didn't want him to know because he'd have come into my room with her to show that there was nothing there.

Sadly there *was* something there – a pair of grey flappy ears, a trunk and half an elephant's head.

"So many odd things have been going on," Sarah said. "There was that awful little fat man I saw and ..."

Then all at once she went silent. I was at the sink, and I turned to see why.

She was silent because she'd vanished!

And just then her friend Helen banged on the door to walk to school with us.

I looked everywhere for Sarah. But I knew what must have happened. It didn't take long to work *that* out.

I shouted to Helen that we'd be with her in a moment, then I ran up to my room (just two elephant ears and one elephant eye left) and tapped out Genie.

"Where is she?" I asked. "Where's Sarah?"

"She's gone away to think things over," Genie said in a grand voice.

"Gone away? Gone away where?"

"She's in the middle of the desert, oh Princess." He bowed. "It is to punish her for calling Genie an awful little fat man again. She must walk across hot sands for 50 days. Then she can come back."

I shook my head. "She'll have to come back before that!" I said. "People will find out she's gone. My dad will go mad!"

"She must be punished, oh Princess," said the Genie.

"I'm sure she must," I said. "But my dad will get the police. And Helen's come for us and we've got to go to school. Sarah will have to come back *now.*"

I spoke in a bossy princess sort of way. Genie gave a sigh. He waved his hands about a bit.

"OK. She is back," he said in a sulk.

I said thanks, tapped him back into the box, and went down to the kitchen. I let Helen in on the way.

In the sitting room, Sarah was watching TV in a dazed sort of way.

"Oh, a programme about life in the desert," I said, and switched it off at once.

"The desert ..." Sarah said in a stunned voice. "Awful hot place ... you could smell the dry sand ..."

I felt like dying on the spot.

"What's up with you?" asked Helen.

"She's just been watching this real-life programme about the desert," I said.

"Nothing but burning sand ..." Sarah droned on.

I poked her to get up. "Come on, then. School!"

Helen looked closely at Sarah. "Some real-life programme," she said. "You've got sand in your hair!"

I froze, then slapped Helen on the back. "Very funny!"

Your time's up, Genie!
VILLAGE EVENTS

"No, really, she has. There, look! I can ..."

I grabbed Sarah's school bag and pushed both of them out of the door. We'd got as far as the gate when I made up my mind. It had been a close thing. *Too* close.

"Just a moment. I've left something behind," I said. I went back into the house and came out with the blue box.

"What have you got *that* for?" Helen asked.

I had made up my mind. It was all very well having Genie, but it was just too much for me to cope with.

I waved the box at her. "I'm going to drop this off at the church," I told her. "It'll just do for their next jumble sale."

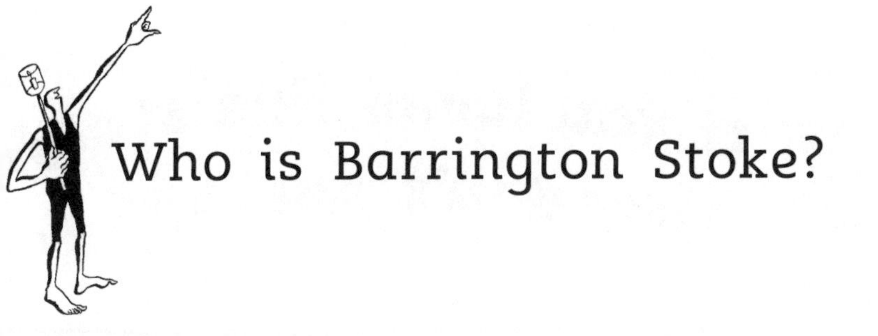

Who is Barrington Stoke?

Barrington Stoke went from place to place with his lamp in his hand. Everywhere he went, he told stories to children. Some were happy, some were sad, some were funny and some were scary.

The children always wanted more. When it got dark, they had to go home to bed. They went to look for Barrington Stoke the next day, but he had gone.

The children never forgot the stories. They told them to each other and to their children and their grandchildren. You see, good stories are magic and they can live for ever.

If you loved this story, why don't you read ...

Living with Vampires

by Jeremy Strong

Are your parents normal? Kevin's parents are really odd. They can turn people into zombies. And worse still, they're coming to the school disco! How can Kevin get his parents to behave normally?

4u2read.ok!

You can order this book directly from our website: www.barringtonstoke.co.uk

If you loved this story, why don't you read ...

Friday Forever

by Annie Dalton

Do you wake up on Monday wishing it was Friday? Lenny does. He's under so much stress it's crazy! Then, one day, Lenny makes a wish by accident and things change – for ever!

4u2read.ok!